Barbie™

Thumbelina

By Sue Kassirer • Illustrated by S.I. Artists

Cover photography by Willy Lew, Shirley Ushirogata, Greg Roccia,
David Westphal, Steve Toth, Judy Tsuno, and Lisa Collins

 A GOLDEN BOOK • NEW YORK

BARBIE and associated trademarks and trade dress are owned by, and used under license from, Mattel, Inc.
Copyright © 2003 Mattel, Inc. All Rights Reserved.
Published in the United States by Golden Books, an imprint of Random House Children's Books, a division
,of Random House, Inc., 1745 Broadway, New York, NY 10019, and in Canada by Random House of Canada
Limited, Toronto. No part of this book may be reproduced or copied in any form without permission
from the copyright owner. Golden Books, A Golden Book, A Little Golden Book, the G colophon, and
the distinctive gold spine are registered trademarks of Random House, Inc.
Library of Congress Control Number: 2002094153   ISBN: 978-0-307-10452-6
www.randomhouse.com/kids
Printed in the United States of America   14 13 12 11 10 9 8 7 6

Once there was a tiny girl no taller
than your thumb. Her name was Thumbelina.

During the day, Thumbelina sang
and sailed her tulip-petal boat.

At night, she slept in a walnut shell.
It had a mattress of violets and a blanket
of rose petals.

One day, an old toad heard Thumbelina singing. "What a beautiful voice she has!" thought the toad. "She'd make a fine wife for my son."

That night, as Thumbelina slept, the mother toad picked up Thumbelina in her pretty bed and carried her off!

When Thumbelina awoke, stranded on a lily pad,
she began to cry.

Some fish heard Thumbelina crying. They knew what the mother toad had in mind. So they bit off the stem of the lily pad, and Thumbelina floated away—far from the toad and her son.

When the lily pad finally swirled to a stop against a bank, Thumbelina made a new home for herself. She wove a hammock from blades of grass. She drank sweet nectar and dew from the buttercups.

But soon autumn came and the flowers died.
Then winter came and it began to snow.
    Thumbelina, now hungry and cold, knocked
on a little door under a snow-covered cornfield.

"Come in, my dear," said a friendly field mouse.
"Make yourself warm. You may live here if you will
clean for me."

So Thumbelina decided to stay, and the two
happily shared the mouse's cozy burrow.

One evening, the mouse's neighbor came to visit.
He was a mole.

"He's rich," hinted the mouse after the mole had
left. But Thumbelina did not care, for the mole disliked
the sun and the flowers. His only wish was to stay
forever underground in the dark.

The mole came to visit more and more, for he liked Thumbelina. He even dug a tunnel between the mouse's home and his own.

One day, Thumbelina found a swallow in the tunnel. It was numb with cold.

"Poor bird," whispered Thumbelina. "Didn't the mole help you?"

She wove the swallow a warm mat of hay, and fed him all winter long. Slowly, she brought him back to health.

When she wasn't caring for the swallow, Thumbelina
spun silk into the fabric for her wedding dress. For the
mole had proposed, and the mouse had decided that
Thumbelina should marry him. Poor Thumbelina
dreaded saying good-bye to the sun and the flowers.

When spring came, the swallow was able to fly!
On her wedding day, Thumbelina said good-bye to
him with tears in her eyes.

"Come with me," begged the swallow. "We'll fly
to a place where it is always warm."

"Yes, I will," said Thumbelina suddenly.
She climbed onto the bird's back and tied a sash
to his feathers.

Away they flew, over mountains and lakes.

When they reached the warm southern lands, the swallow
placed Thumbelina on a soft flower petal. And there, in
the heart of the flower, stood a handsome little man. He was
the king of the flowers.

The two fell instantly in love.

Soon afterward, Thumbelina married the king. And as a gift, the people of the flower kingdom gave Thumbelina her very own wings, so that she could fly with the king from flower to flower.